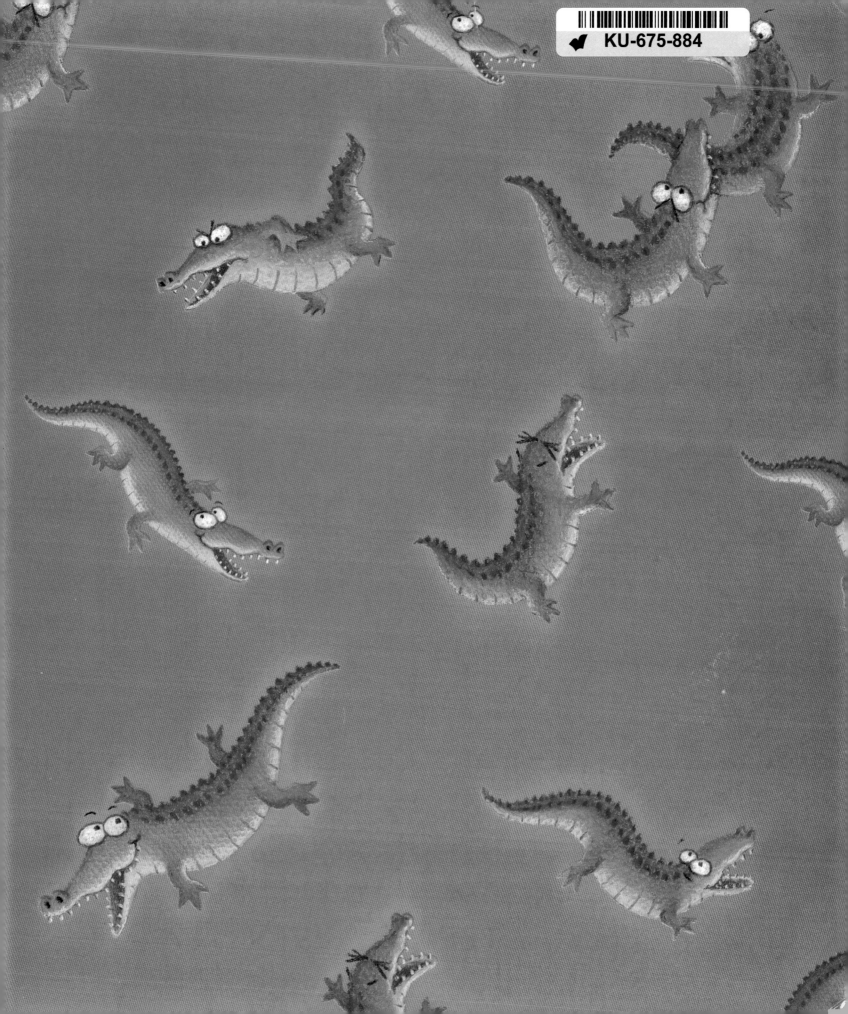

To Janet and Sam –
who know what this is all about. With love, Tom

For Yuta and Kenta and all their teeth! L.C.

First published in the United Kingdom in 2004
by Chrysalis Children's Books, an imprint of Chrysalis Books Group plc
The Chrysalis Building
Bramley Road
London W10 6SP
This paperback edition first published in 2005

Text copyright © 2004 Tom Barber.
Illustrations copyright © 2004 Lynne Chapman.

Tom Barber asserts his moral right to be
identified as the author of this work.
Lynne Chapman asserts her moral right to be
identified as the illustrator of this work.

Designed by Sarah Goodwin and Keren-Orr Greenfeld

BRITISH LIBRARY CATALOGUING-IN-PUBLICATION DATA
A catalogue record for this book is available from the British Library.

ISBN 1 85602 505 5 (hardback)
ISBN 1 84458 053 9 (paperback)
Printed in China.

OPEN WIDE!

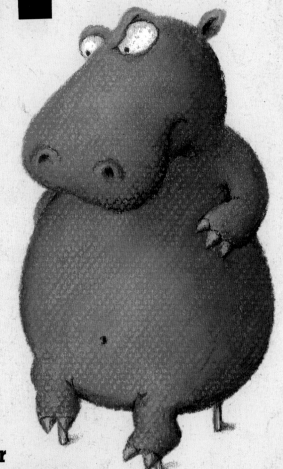

Tom Barber
Illustrated by Lynne Chapman

Chrysalis Children's Books

Sam did not like going to the dentist, not one little bit. Yes, the waiting room had a fish tank and he got a sticker and a treat from Dad afterwards, but that was not nearly enough to make it all right.

"Good morning, Sam," said Mr Murgatroyd, the dentist.
Sam looked at the bright light overhead...
the funny chair that looked like it
might close on you with a snap...
and the tray of pointy metal
things on the little table.

Sam felt Dad let go of his arm. Now was his chance. Sam made a dash for it...

"Come out this second, Sam," said Dad.
"No," growled Sam.

"Leave it to me, Mr Spurr," said Mr Murgatroyd. And before Sam knew what was happening, the dentist had squeezed under the chair with him.

"You know, Sam, you'd be amazed at some of the teeth I have to look at."

"This morning I had a full-grown tiger in here.
I pretended I wasn't scared," said Mr Murgatroyd.
Sam pretended he wasn't listening.
"There was a thread jammed
between two of his back teeth.
I grabbed it with my pincers
and wiggled it free."

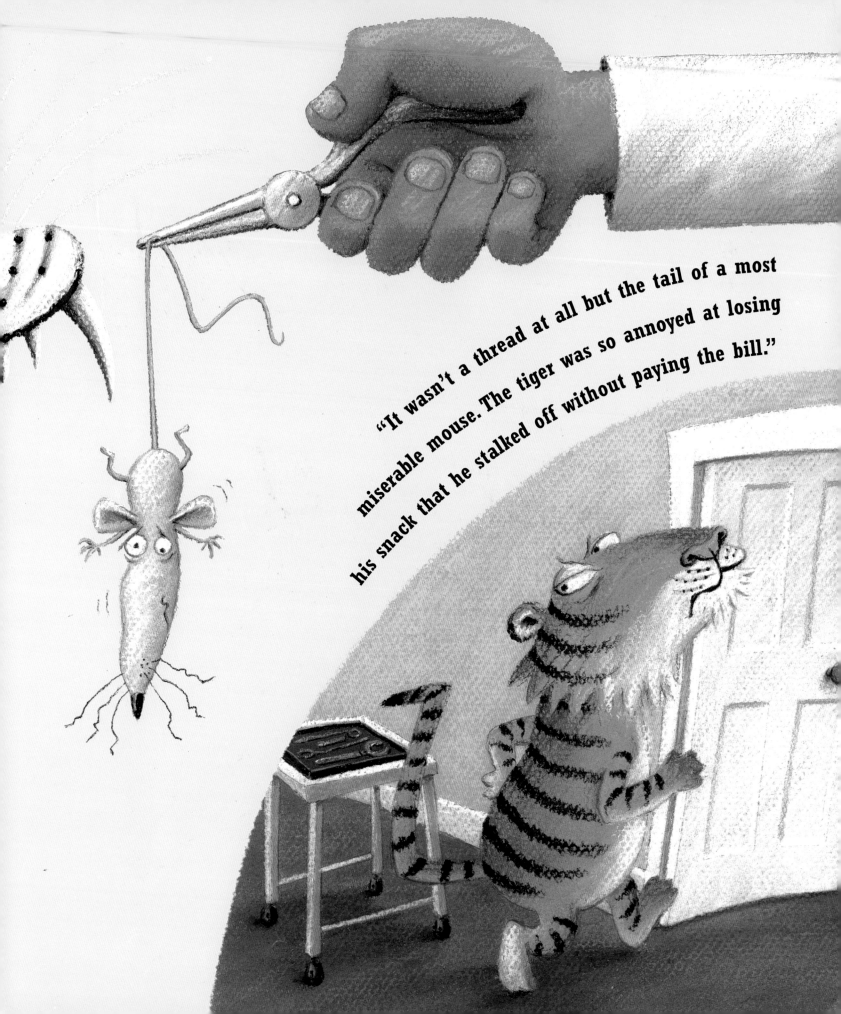

"It wasn't a thread at all but the tail of a most miserable mouse. The tiger was so annoyed at losing his snack that he stalked off without paying the bill."

"And that's not all," went on Mr Murgatroyd. "See that hole there? An old nanny goat did that. Goats will chew anything and she had already worn out eight pairs of false teeth."

"The only way I could stop her eating the rest of the chair was to promise her a new set made of gold. She was very pleased with them."

"And the week before that, you'll never believe it – a hippo with toothache! He was even more grumpy than usual. What a massive mouth! I could have climbed right inside."

"One of his front teeth had a big crack in it. It had to come out, of course. I told him he must stop biting boats, but I bet he won't take any notice."

"Do you want to see the tooth?" Sam nodded.

"The Thursday before that we had a visit from a beaver."
"Blunt teeth?" asked Sam, who knew a thing or two about animals.
"How did you guess?" asked Mr Murgatroyd. "I gave them a good
sharpen with the tooth file. He was very grateful, but he would
insist on trying them out before he left."

"Then last month a crocodile arrived at the door.
'We've just come for a check up,' she said very politely.
'We?' I asked. She opened her mouth and then I understood."
"Her babies?" said Sam.

"Exactly," said Mr Murgatroyd. "Every one of
their nine hundred and sixty-six teeth were
fine but they all wanted the same sticker
so there was a bit of a squabble."

"Do you want to choose your sticker now?"

"Yes, please," said Sam.

"Take two if you like."

He took three but Mr Murgatroyd didn't seem to notice.

"Who else?" asked Sam.

"Well now, I don't normally do beaks, but I couldn't refuse a poor toucan.
She had eaten too many overripe mangoes and flown smack into a tree trunk.
A twist with the pincers, a splint and a bandage and that was that."

"If you come and sit in the chair you can see the feathers she gave me," Mr Murgatroyd said. "They're beautiful," said Sam, "and look, she's laid an egg up there as well."

"What's the biggest animal you've ever looked at?" said Sam. "A humpback whale," said Mr Murgatroyd. "He had been set upon by a pack of hammerhead sharks. They had bashed big holes in his teeth so he couldn't eat properly. It was a sorry business. I bent so many of my tools fixing them I had to buy some new ones. Shall I show you?"

"And what about the scariest?" asked Sam,
when he could move his mouth again.
"That would have to be the spitting cobra,"
said Mr Murgatroyd.

"He's so deadly poisonous, I had to wear chainmail gloves just in case he bit me by mistake. And when it was time for him to rinse and spit in the basin we all had to leave the room."

"You can have a rinse now, Sam. Pink or blue water?" "Blue please," said Sam.

"What with tigers, goats, hippopotamuses, crocodiles, beavers, toucans, whales and cobras, you're the best patient I've had in that chair for weeks, Sam. Off you go, we're all finished."

"Already? Can I keep the hippo's tooth?" asked Sam.
"Only if you promise to bring it back with you next time you come."
"I will," said Sam, and he showed it to Dad on the way out.

"I didn't believe any of those stories, did you?" said Sam.
"No, of course not," said Dad. "Though I'm not sure where that hippo's tooth came from... Now, are you ready for the monster movie?"